W9-CEW-187

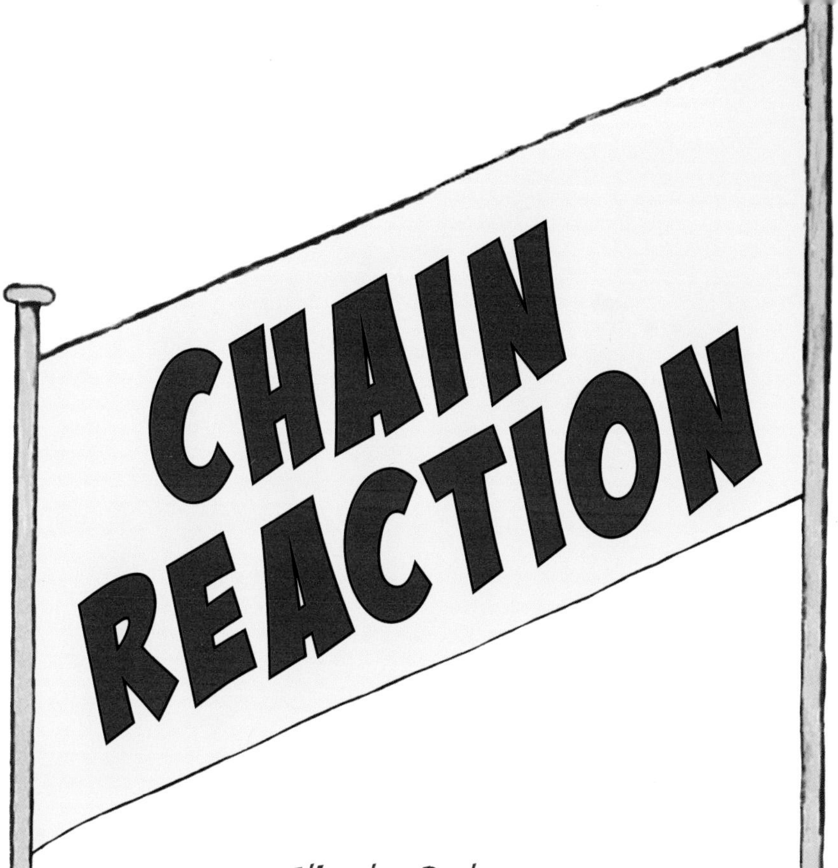
CHAIN
REACTION

Librarian Reviewer

Chris Kreie

Media Specialist, Eden Prairie Schools, MN

MS in Information Media, St. Cloud State University, MN

Reading Consultant

Mary Evenson

Middle School Teacher, Edina Public Schools, MN

MA in Education, University of Minnesota

First published in the United States in 2008
by Stone Arch Books
151 Good Counsel Drive, P.O. Box 669
Mankato, Minnesota 56002
www.stonearchbooks.com

First published by Evans Brothers Ltd
2A Portman Mansions, Chiltern Street
London W1U 6NR, United Kingdom

Library of Congress Cataloging-in-Publication Data
Lawrie, Robin.
    Chain Reaction / by Robin and Chris Lawrie; illustrated by Robin
Lawrie.
    p. cm. — (Ridge Riders)
    Summary: After hurt feelings result in a calamitous crash in the
downhill race, the Ridge Riders learn the importance of working together
as a team.
    ISBN 978-1-4342-0483-7 (library binding)
    ISBN 978-1-4342-0543-8 (paperback)
    [1. All terrain cycling—Fiction. 2. Bicycle racing—Fiction.
3. Teamwork (Sports)—Fiction. 4. Sportsmanship—Fiction. 5. Cartoons
and comics.] I. Lawrie, Christine. II. Title.
PZ7.L438218Cf 2008
[Fic]—dc22   2007029140

1 2 3 4 5 6 13 12 11 10 09 08

Printed in the United States of America

CHAIN REACTION

by Robin and Chris Lawrie
illustrated by Robin Lawrie

STONE ARCH BOOKS
MINNEAPOLIS   SAN DIEGO

The Ridge Riders

 Hi, my name is "Slam" Duncan.

This is Aziz.  We call him Dozy.

Then there's Larry.

This is Fiona.

And Andy.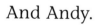

I'm Andy. (Andy is deaf. He uses sign language instead of talking.)

Andy is also known as Handy Andy. He is one of the fastest riders around. He can't hear, so he talks to us using sign language.

We all have sign names that Andy made up for us.

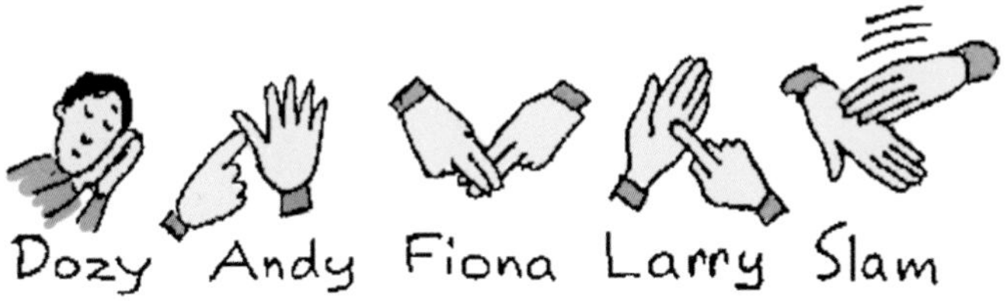
Dozy
Andy
Fiona
Larry
Slam

We all think he's so fast because, since he is deaf, he has fewer distractions when he's racing.

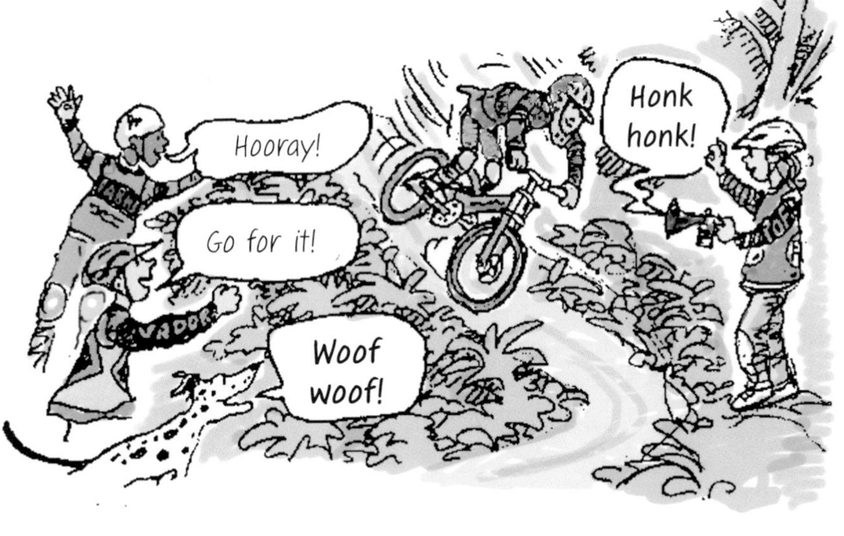
Hooray!
Go for it!
Woof woof!
Honk honk!

Saturday morning. 6 o'clock.

It was the beginning of the Westland Super Series. There would be six races over the next few weeks. The first two would be this weekend. We had camped overnight and it had rained very hard.

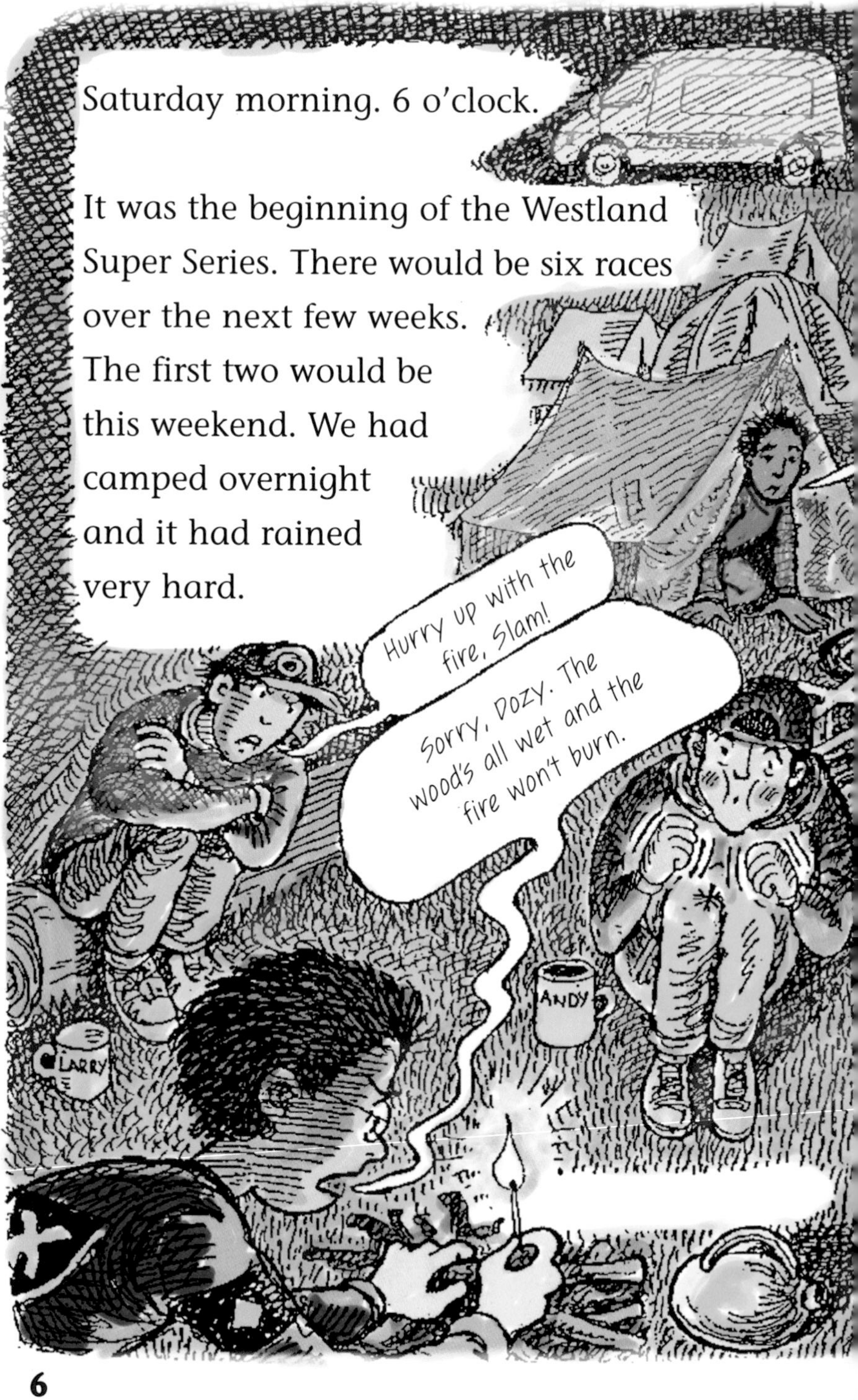
Hurry up with the fire, Slam!
Sorry, Dozy. The wood's all wet and the fire won't burn.
ANDY
LARRY

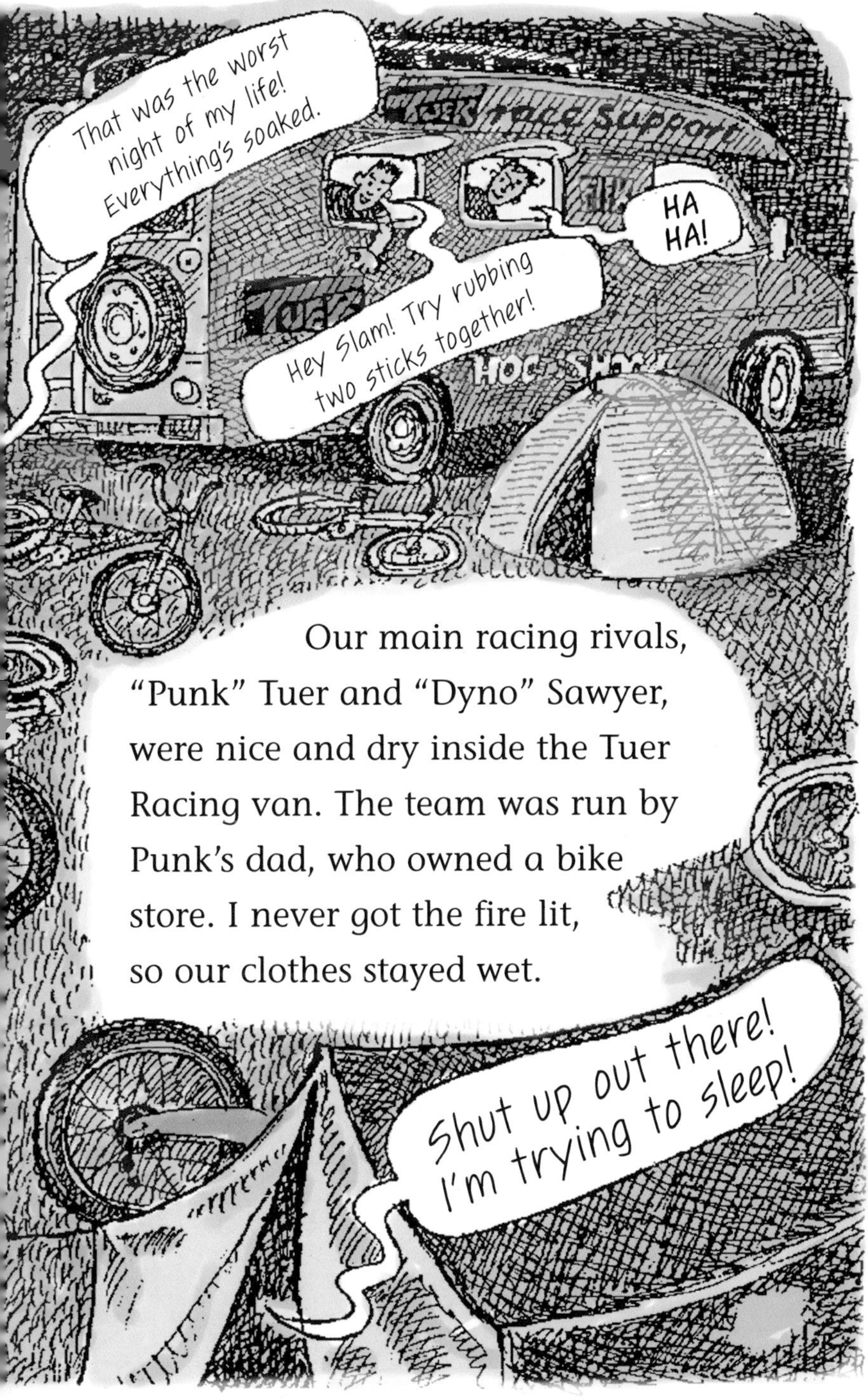
That was the worst night of my life! Everything's soaked.
Hey Slam! Try rubbing two sticks together!
HA HA!
Shut up out there! I'm trying to sleep!

Our main racing rivals, "Punk" Tuer and "Dyno" Sawyer, were nice and dry inside the Tuer Racing van. The team was run by Punk's dad, who owned a bike store. I never got the fire lit, so our clothes stayed wet.

8 o'clock. Race practice on the course. I was riding on smooth tires, which were hopeless on the wet track. I'd let Fiona use my good mud tires, but she was still asleep in her tent. I was having a hard time staying up. Then something awful happened.

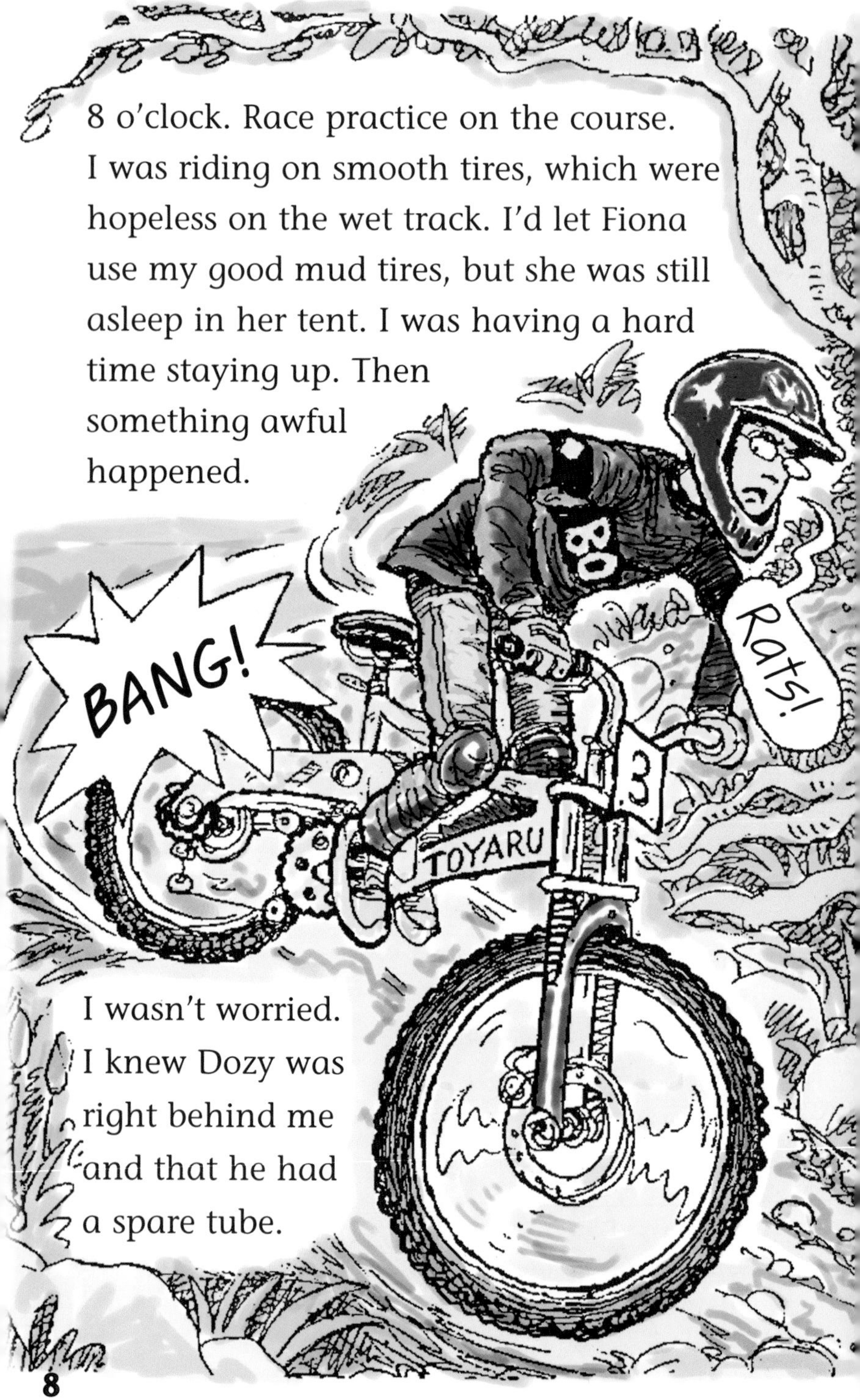
BANG!
Rats!
TOYARU
3

I wasn't worried. I knew Dozy was right behind me and that he had a spare tube.

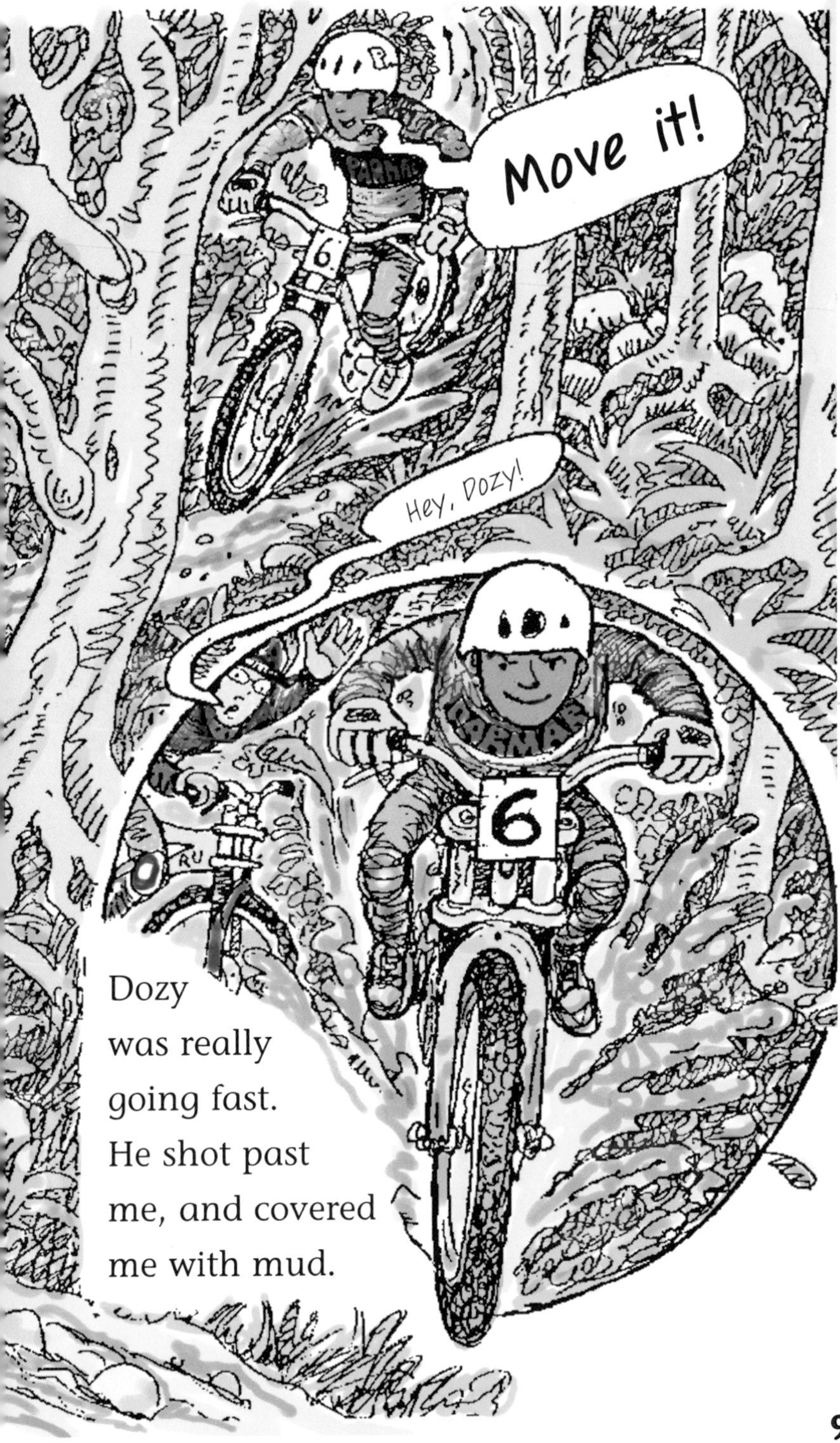
Move it!
Hey, Dozy!

Dozy
was really
going fast.
He shot past
me, and covered
me with mud.

I was sitting and watching the mud drip off me, thinking about how to get back at Dozy, when Andy came zooming down the course. He was going way too fast.

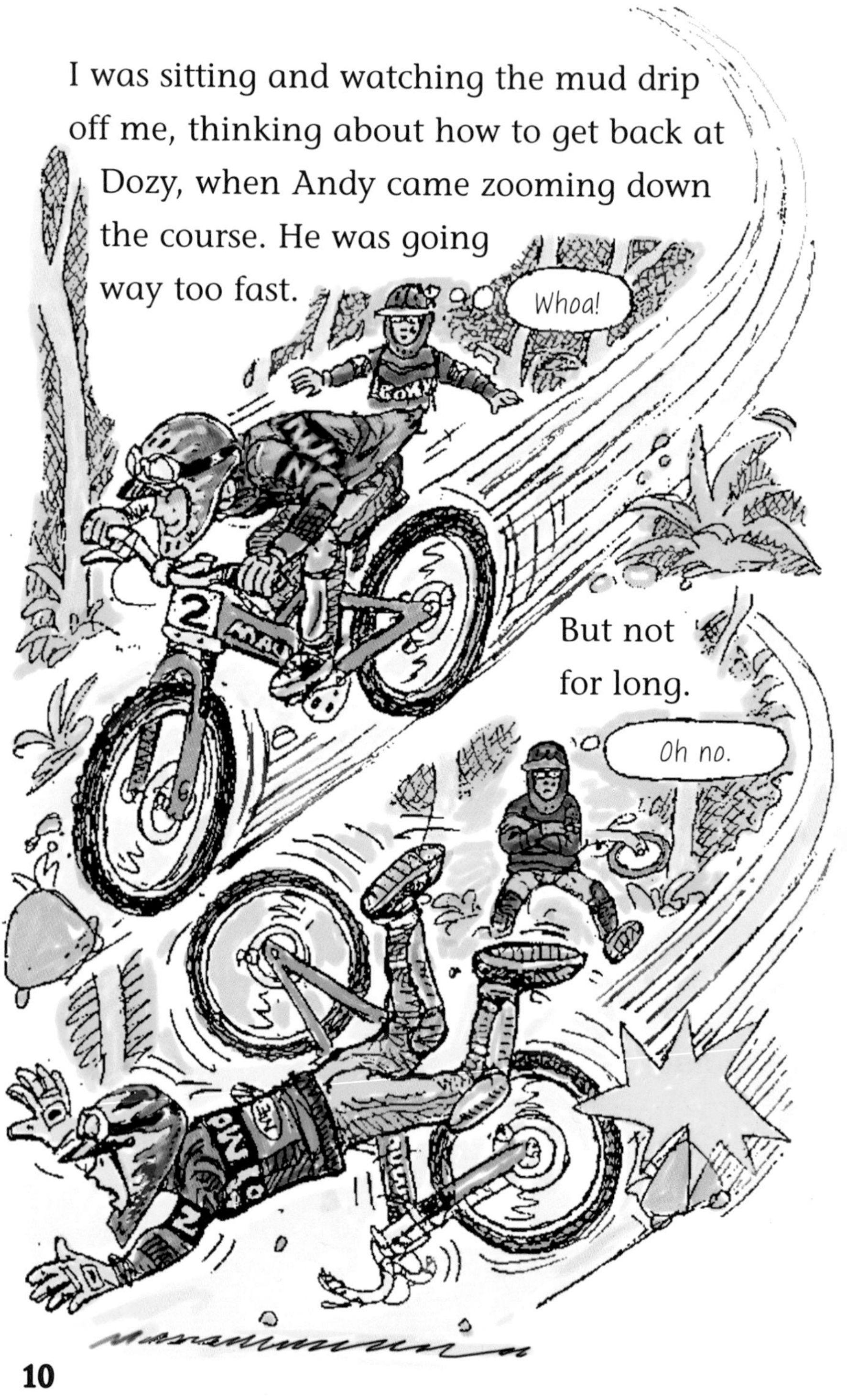
Whoa!
Oh no.

But not for long.

Andy was okay. But his bike wasn't.

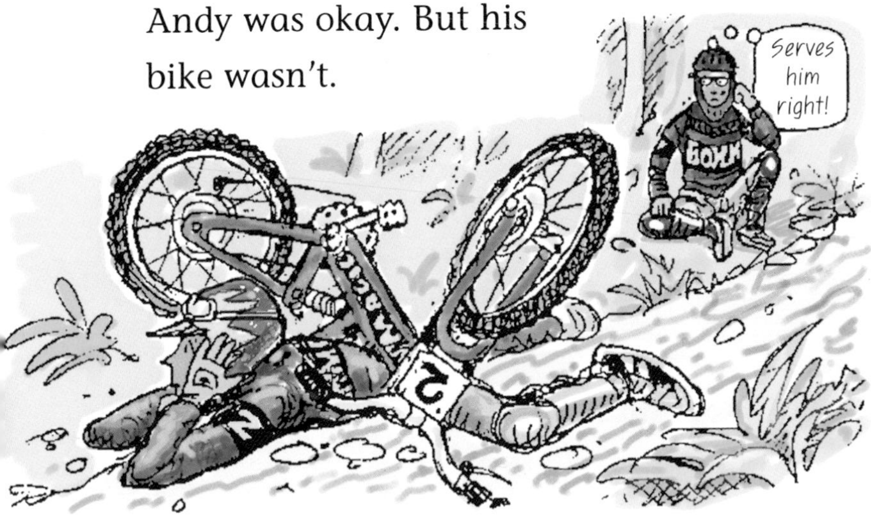
Serves him right!

I was so angry with Dozy that when Andy asked if I had any tools to fix his broken brakes . . .

I just said, "No!"

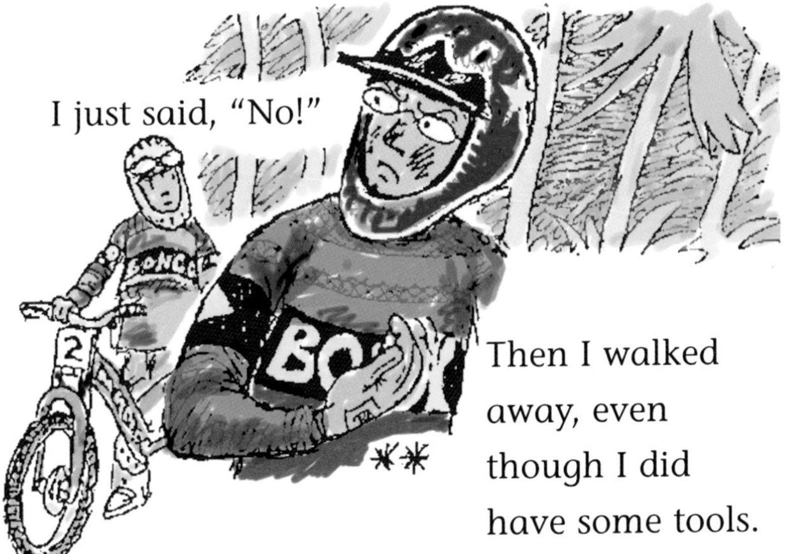

Then I walked away, even though I did have some tools.

Larry had gotten lost, as usual, and as I left to look for a spare tube, I saw him ride up to Andy and ask where the course started.

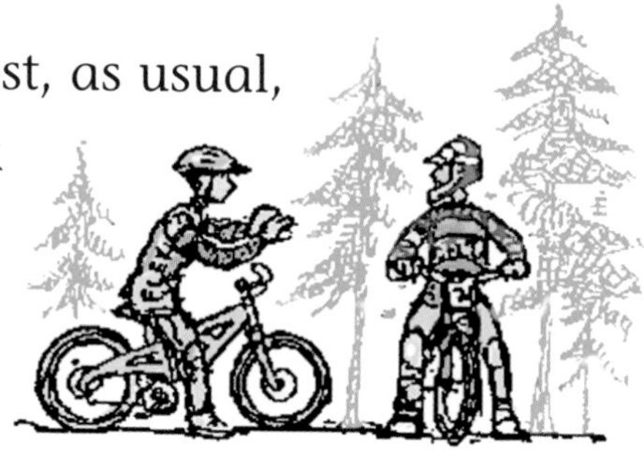

But now Andy was angry too. He pointed down a nearby path where we both knew a farmer lived. The farmer did not like bikers at all.

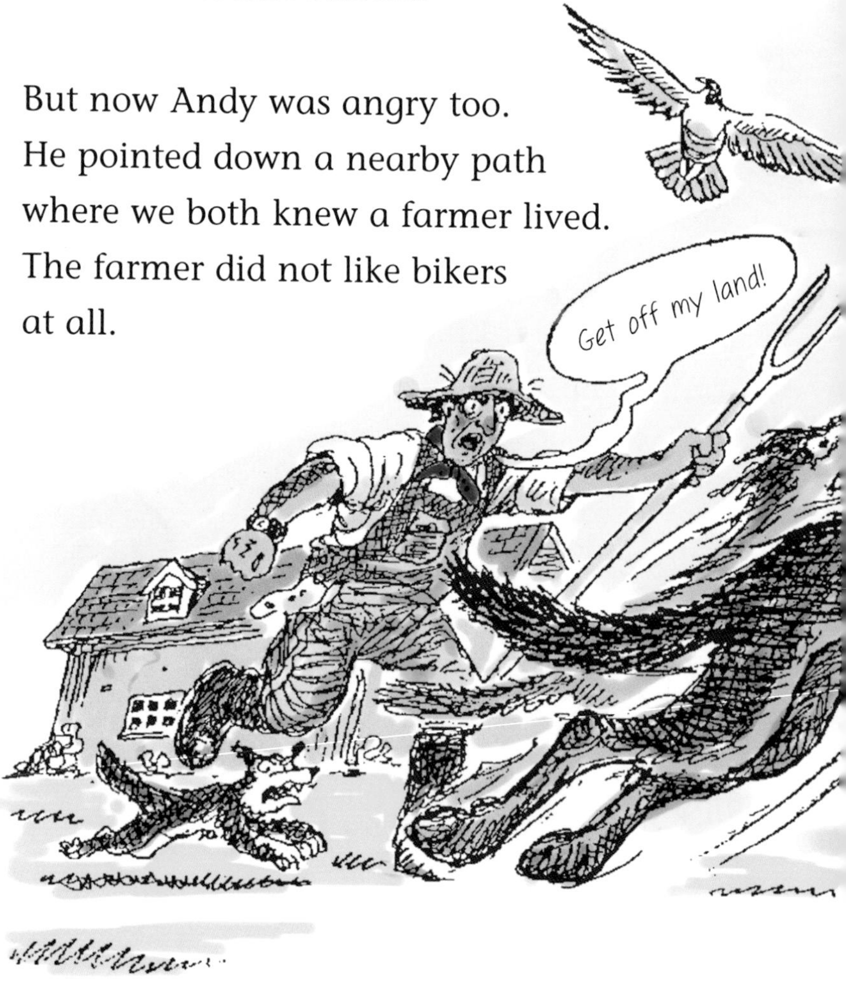
Get off my land!

That wasn't good news for Larry.

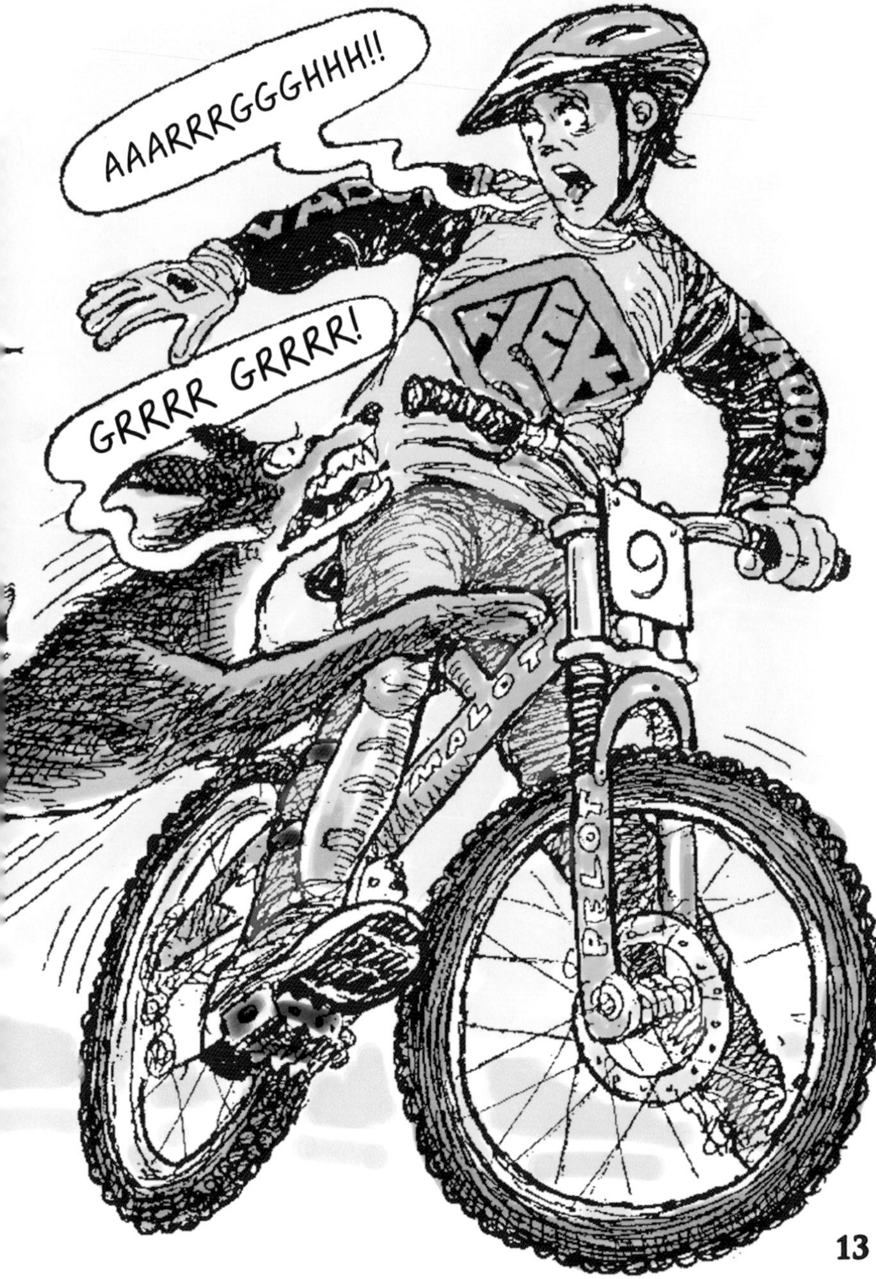
AAARRRGGGHHH!!
GRRRR GRRRR!

Larry must have found the course, because later I saw him practicing — but not very well. He looked like the dog had gotten him. Fiona had finally woken up. She was practicing too. She was coming up behind Larry really fast.

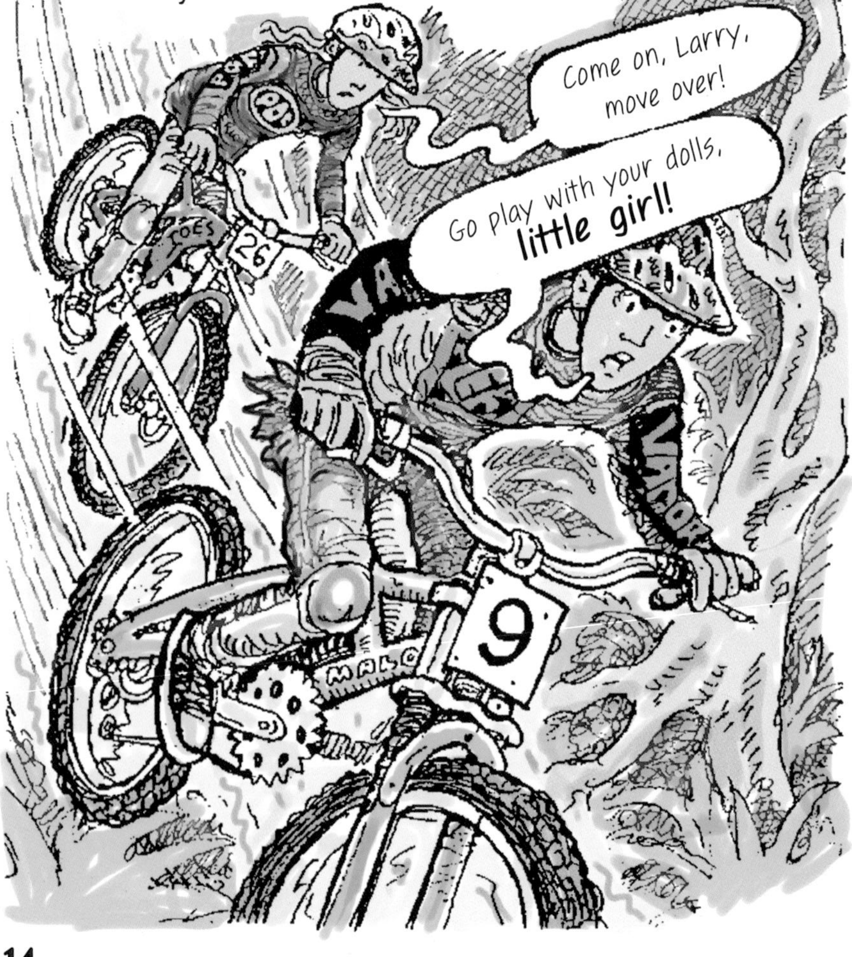

Come on, Larry, move over!
Go play with your dolls, **little girl!**
26
9

Fiona was really upset. She hadn't played with dolls for years. So when I walked up and asked . . .

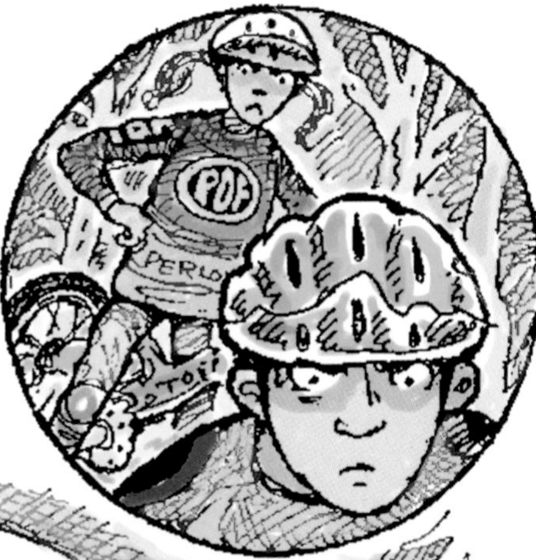

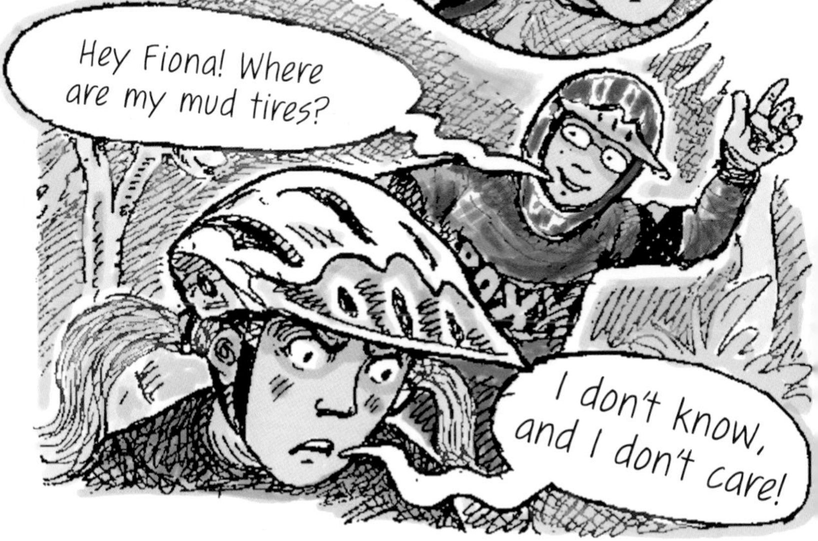
Hey Fiona! Where are my mud tires?
I don't know, and I don't care!

I was mad.

Then Dozy found me. I was still mad at him.

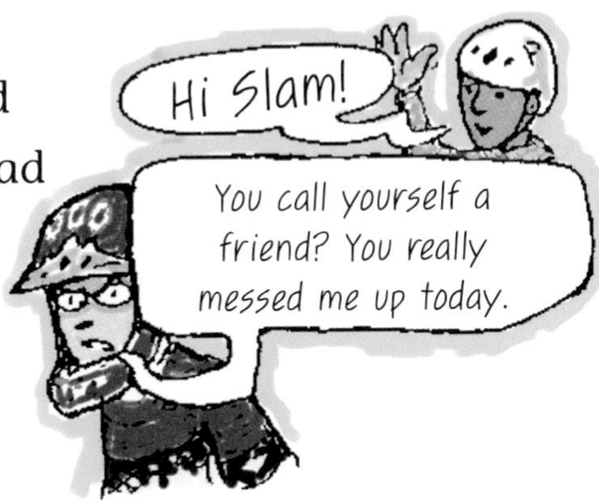
Hi Slam!
You call yourself a friend? You really messed me up today.

I turned around to talk to him.

Now everyone in the Ridge Riders was in a bad mood, and our riding showed it during our first timed run of the day.

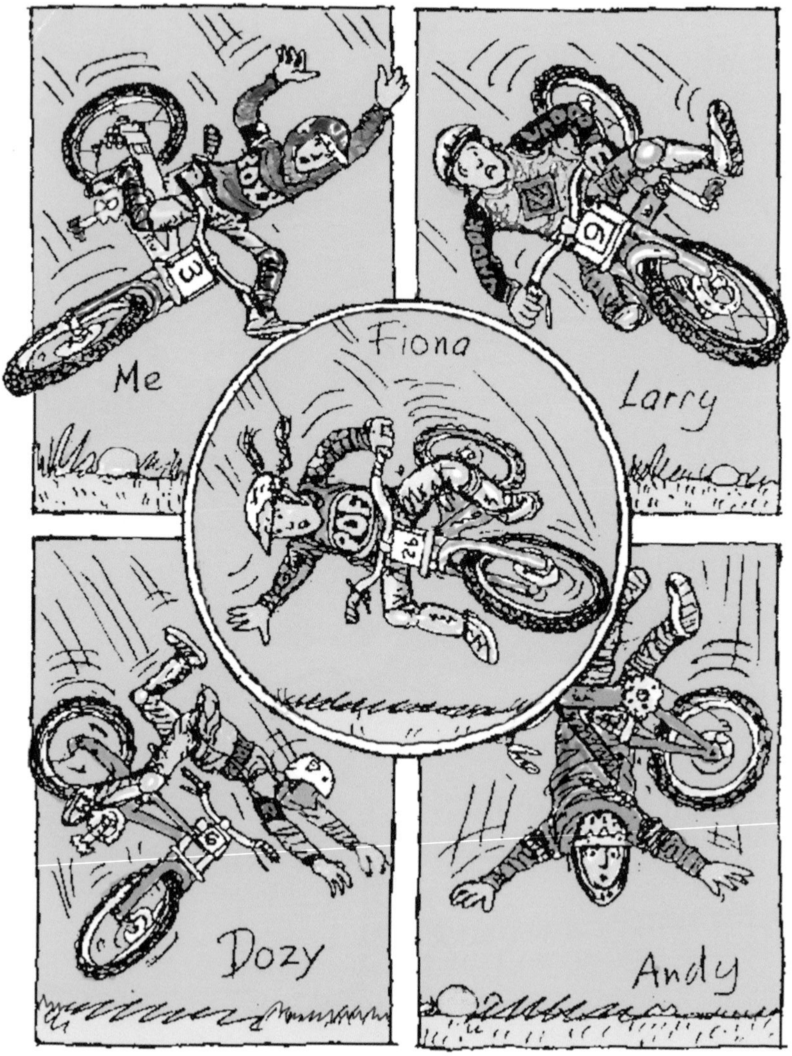
Me
Fiona
Larry
Dozy
Andy

The second run wasn't any better.

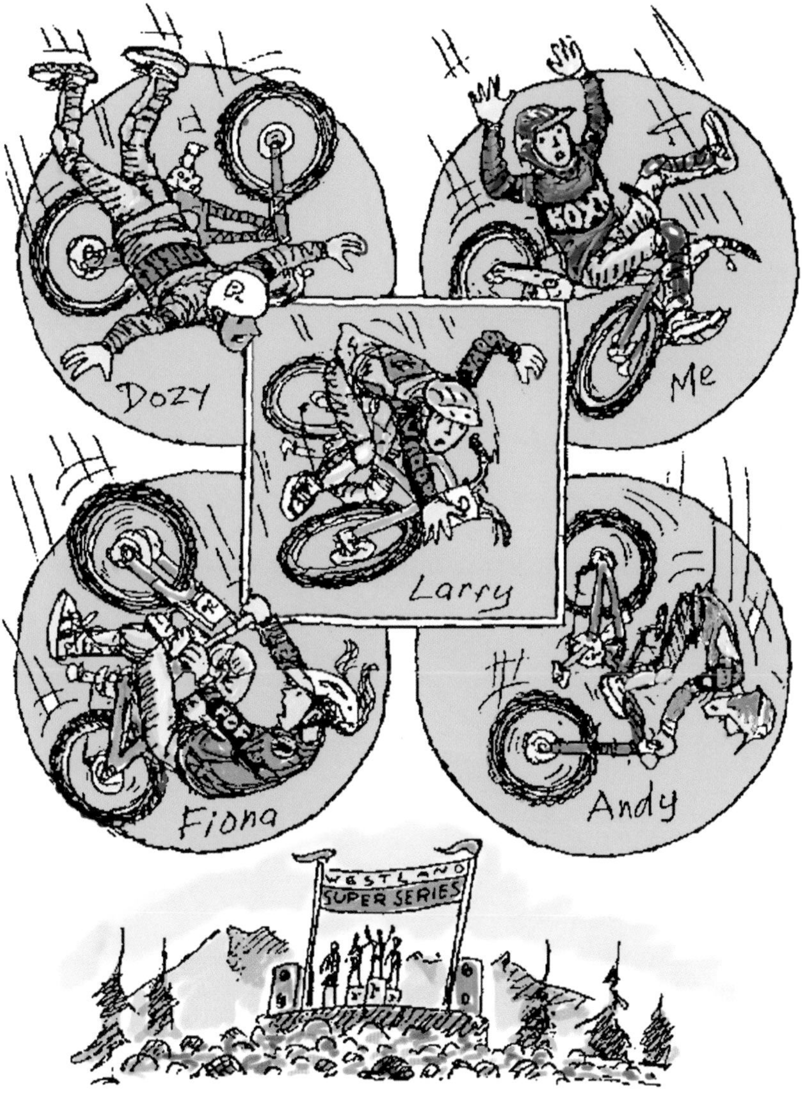
Dozy
Me
Larry
Fiona
Andy
WESTLAND
SUPER SERIES

As a result, Tuer Racing got the first and second fastest times that day.

Sunday morning was bright and sunny, but we were still mad at each other.

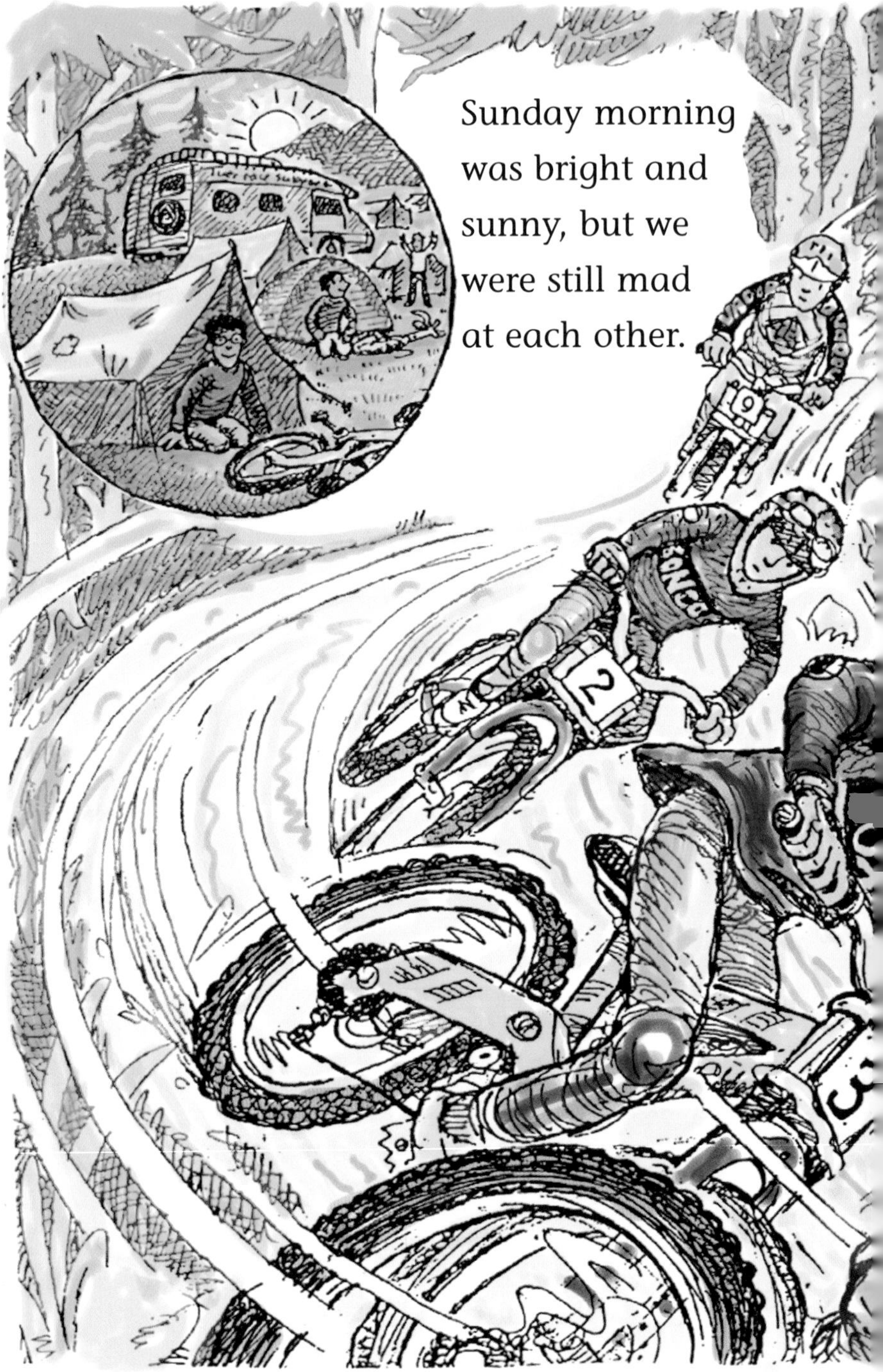

The five of us got out on the course early to practice. In the race, I was determined to beat my friends. So I really went for it. I guess the others felt the same.

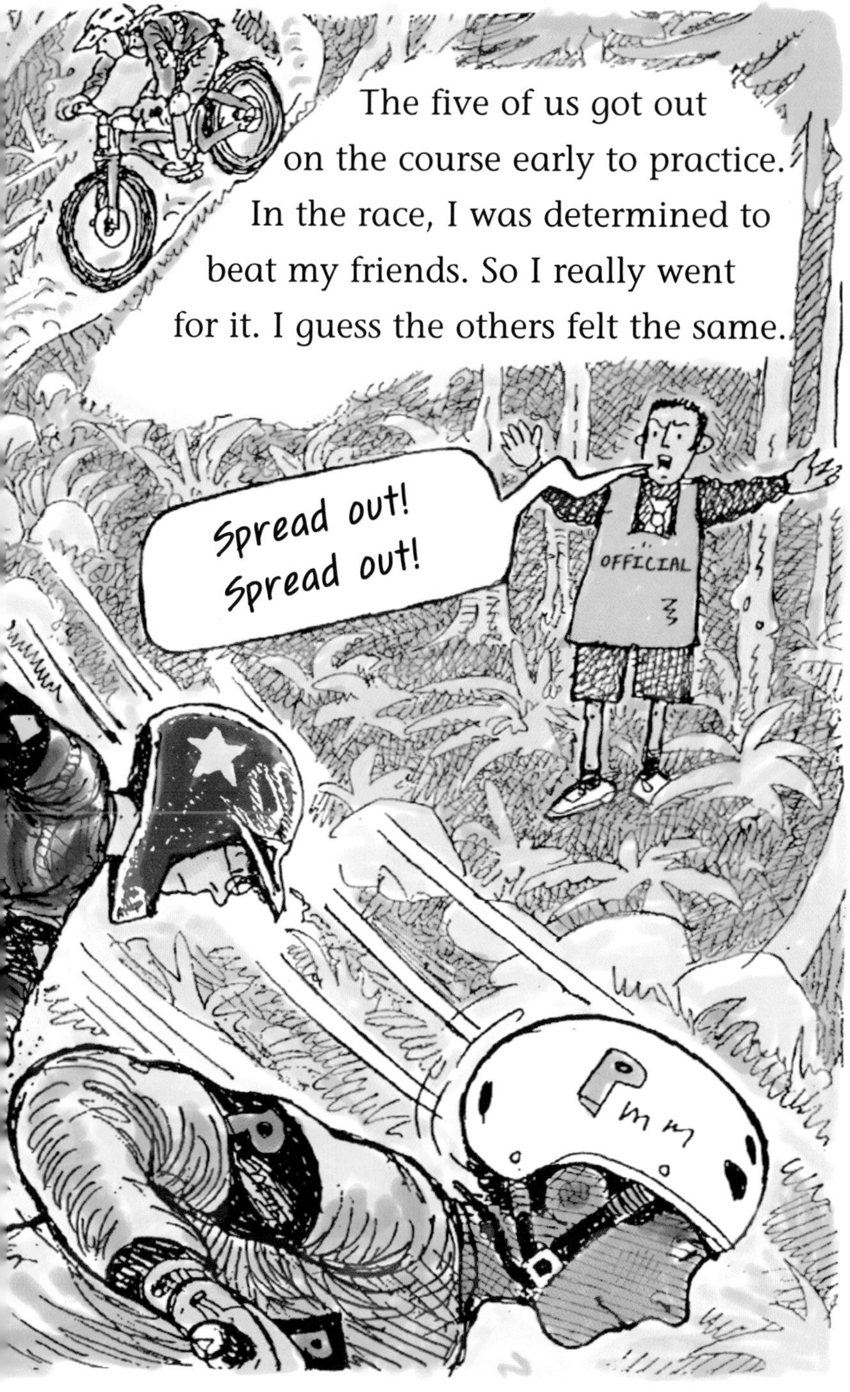
Spread out!
Spread out!
OFFICIAL

That's why it happened:

The Chain Reaction

A. Dozy's chain breaks and he crashes.

B. Slam misses Dozy, but messes up his wheel.

C. Andy shoots into Dozy's bike and gets a flat.

D. Larry falls off and hurts his arm.

E. Fiona brakes so hard that she breaks a cable on her bike.

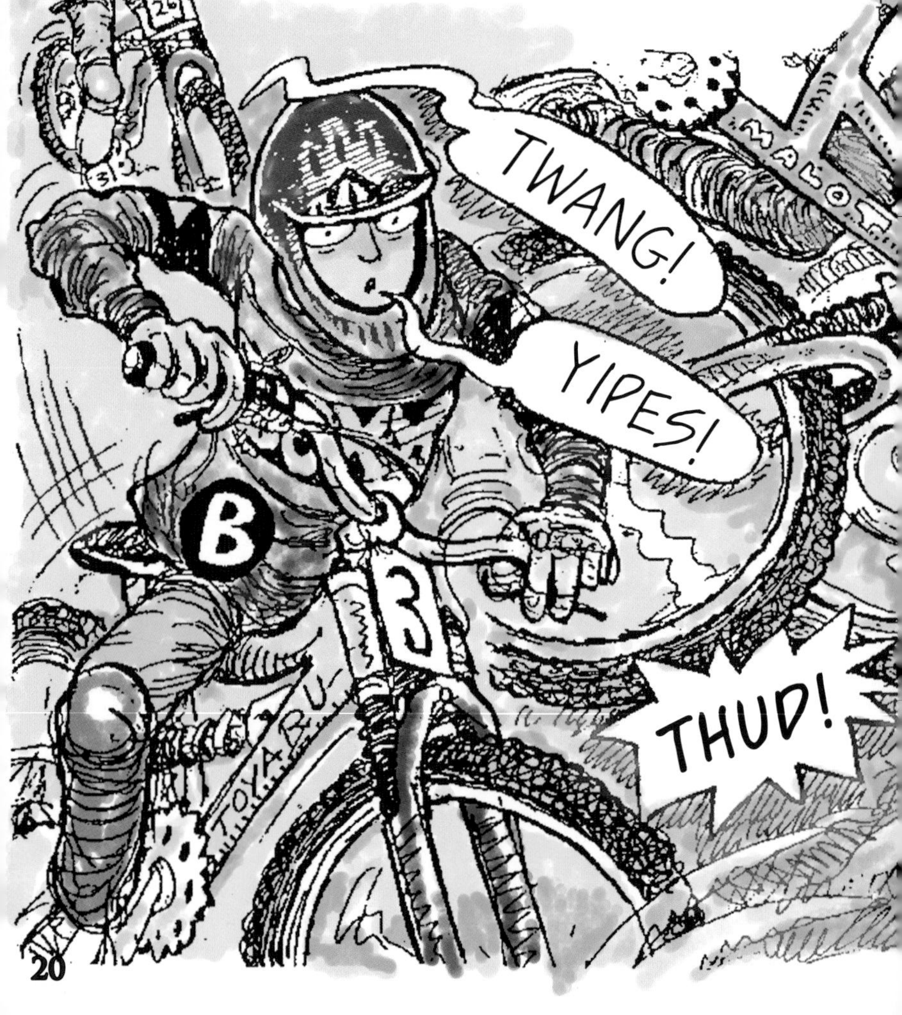
E
B
TWANG!
YIPES!
THUD!

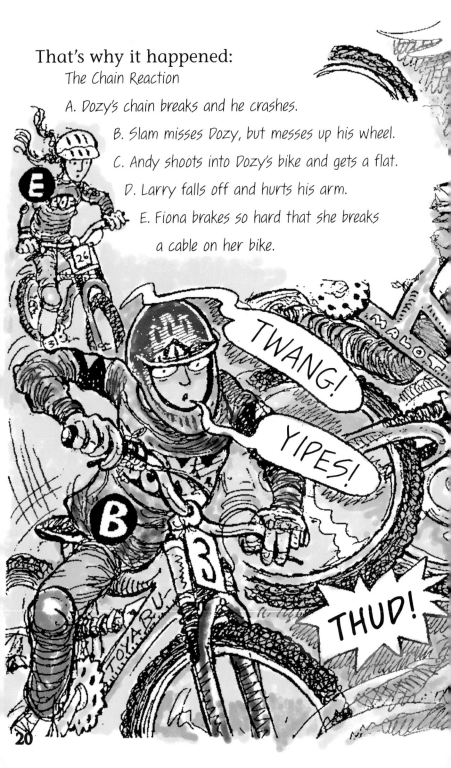

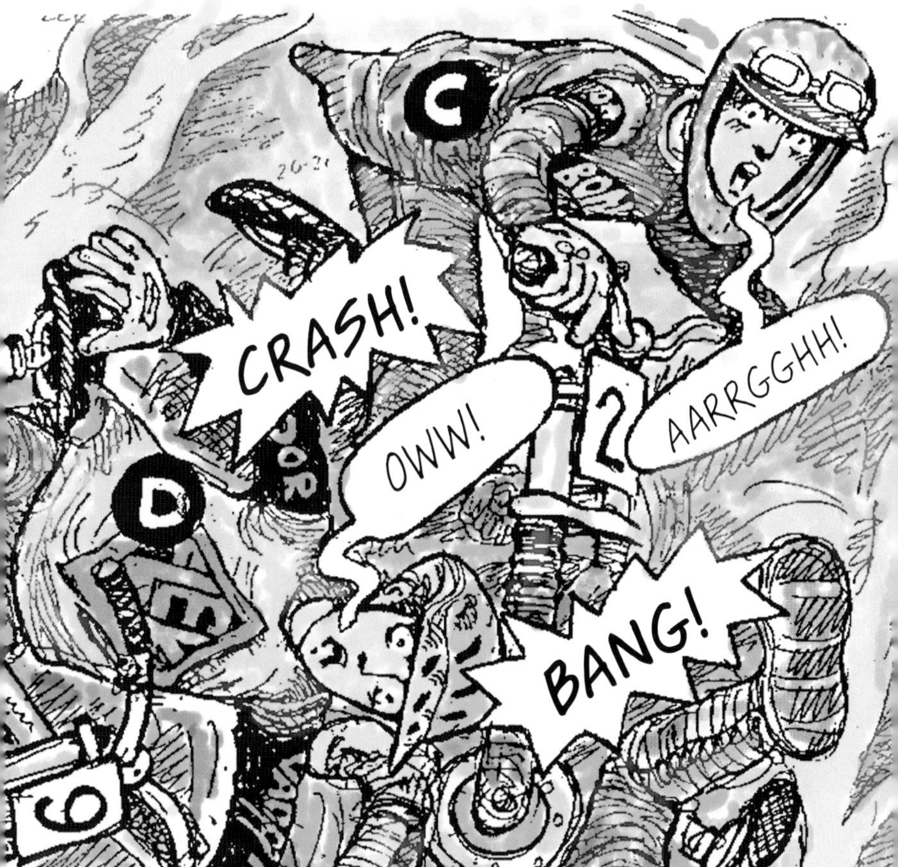
CRASH!
OWW!
AARRGGHH!
BANG!
OUCH!

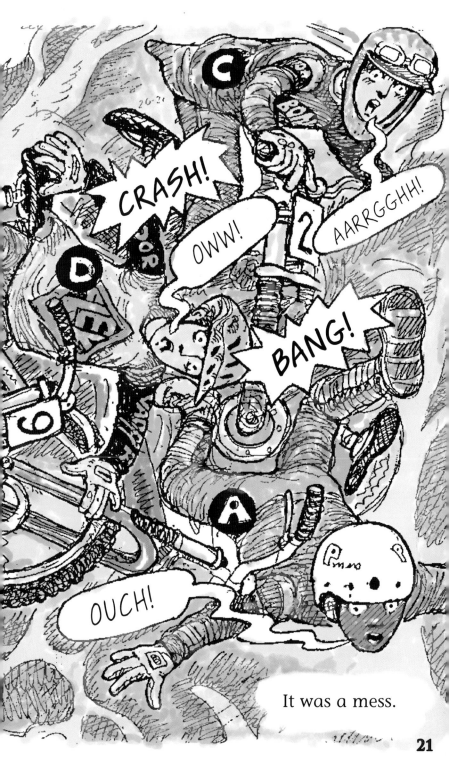

It was a mess.

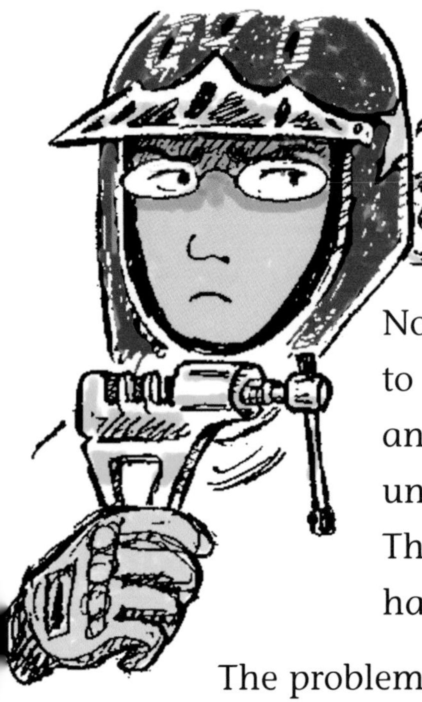

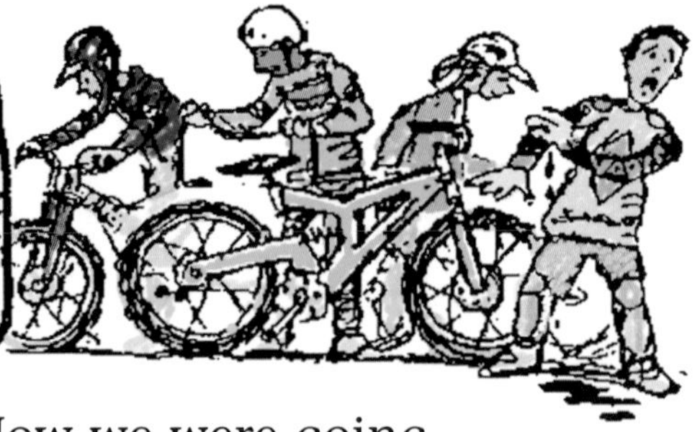

Now we were going to miss our first run, and the second one, too, unless things were fixed. Then I remembered. I had a tool to fix chains.

The problem was, if I fixed Dozy's chain, what was in it for me?

Then I thought about how the Ridge Riders were like one long chain. If one of our links was broken, the whole chain was useless.

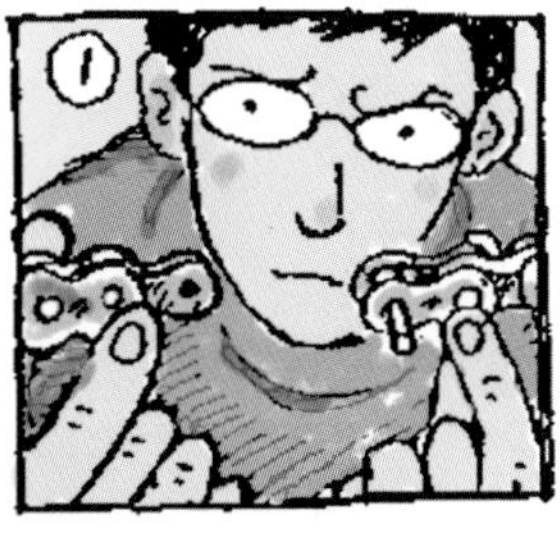
1

So I fixed the link on Dozy's chain.

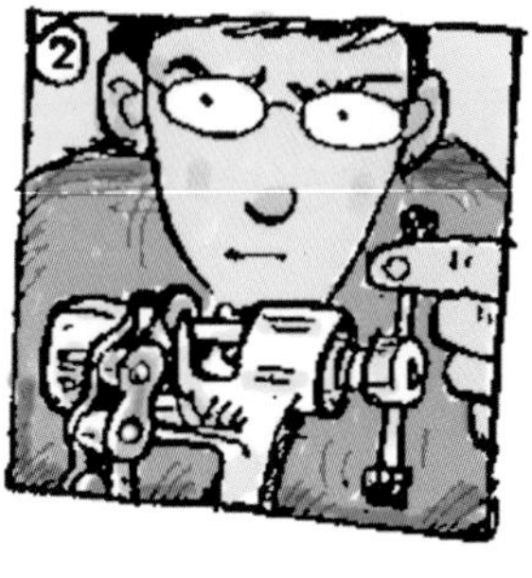
2

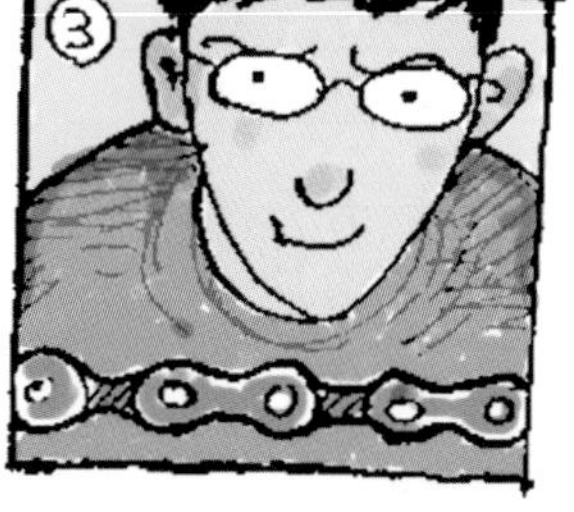
3

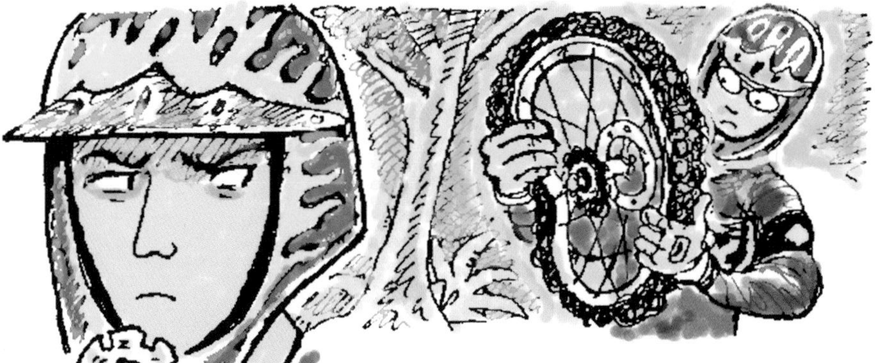

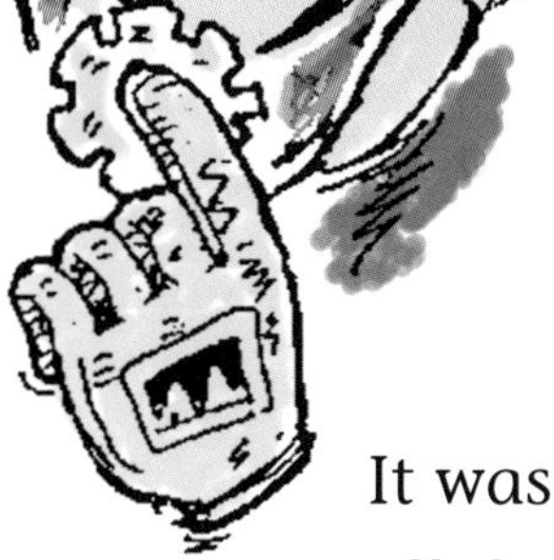

Then Andy dug in his bike bag and pulled out a shiny new spoke tool.

It was the prettiest thing I'd seen all day.

He worked his way around the spokes, tightening some and loosening others. Soon, my wheel was a lot straighter than it had ever been.

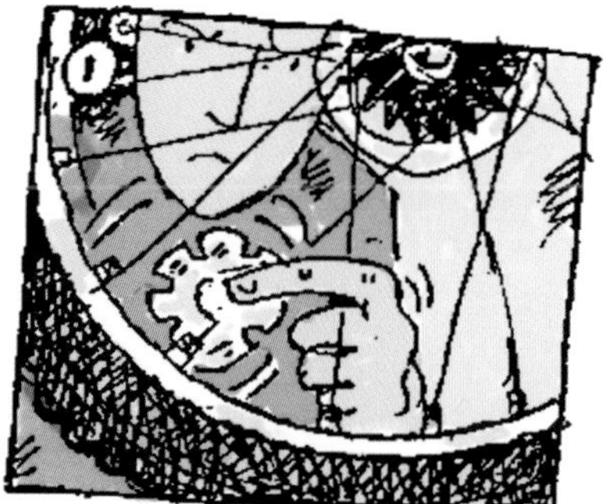
1

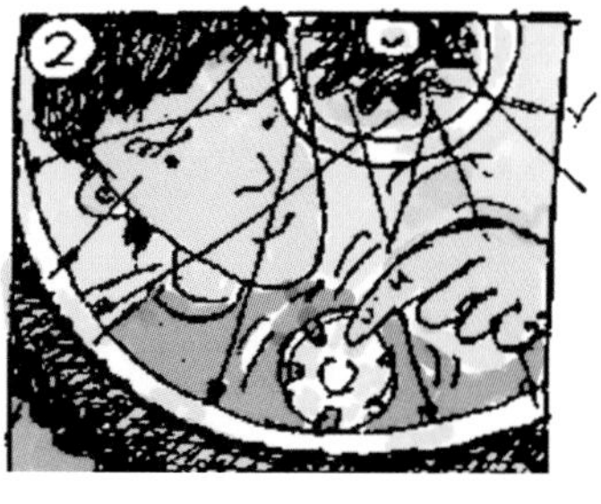
2

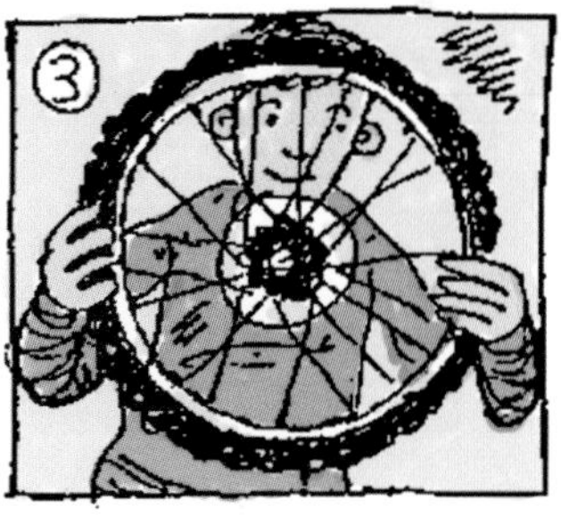
3

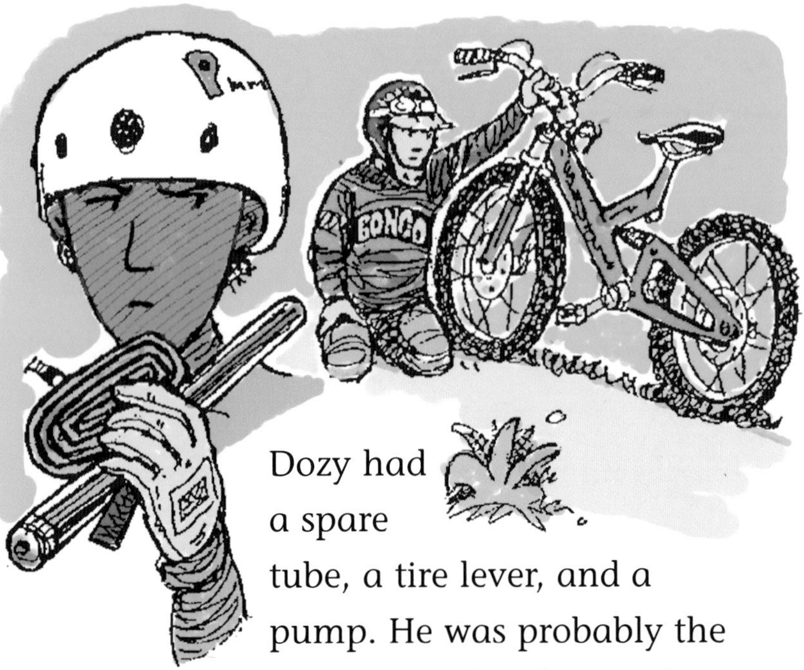

Dozy had a spare tube, a tire lever, and a pump. He was probably the only bike rider I knew who carried all that stuff.

He pulled Andy's tire off with the lever, put in the spare tube, and pumped it up for him.

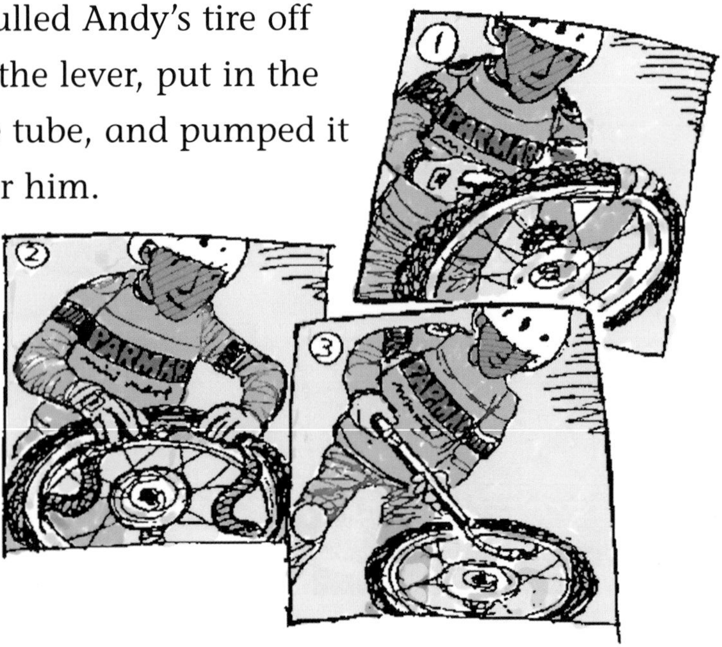
1
2
3

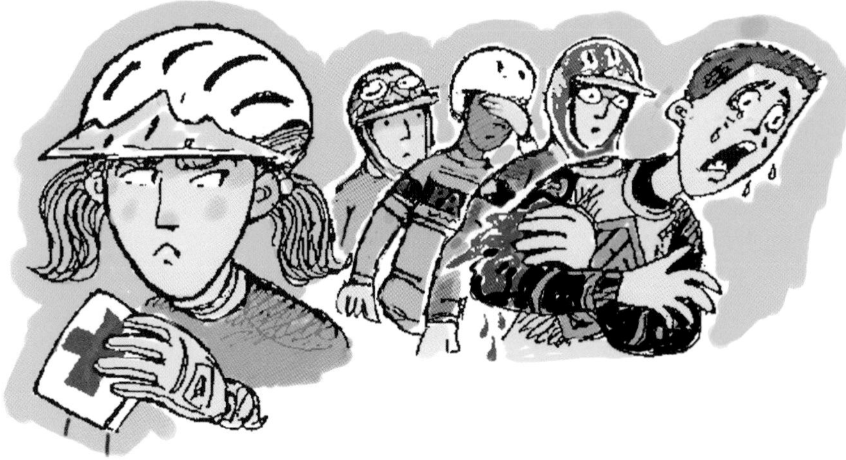

Larry said his arm was really hurting.
Lucky for him, Fiona had a first aid kit.
She cleaned the wound with some wipes.
Then she put a bandage on it.

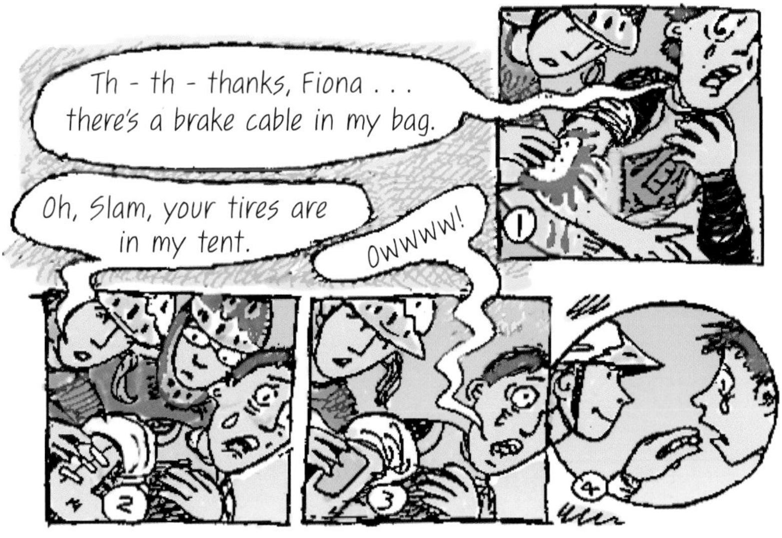

Th - th - thanks, Fiona . . . there's a brake cable in my bag.
Oh, Slam, your tires are in my tent.
OWWWW!

Then she gave Larry a piece of candy to shut him up.

We made it to the top just in time for the second run. Punk and Dyno had both had a terrible first run, so we still had a good chance.

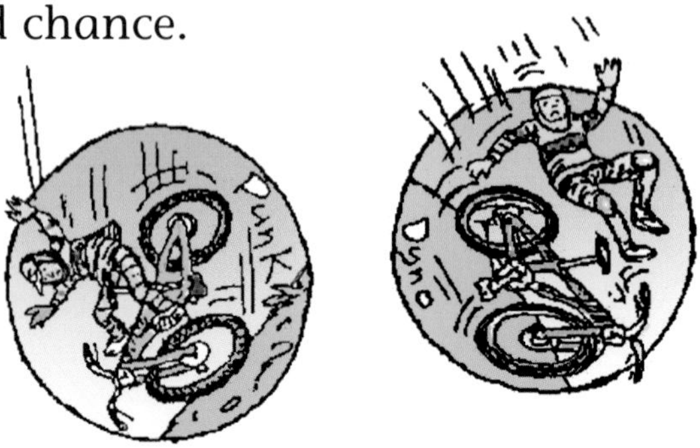
PUNK
Dyno

Downhill bike racing is racing against the clock to see who is the fastest down a steep, rocky, rooty, hillside course. The riders leave the start every 30 seconds. It usually only takes two or three minutes to get to the bottom.

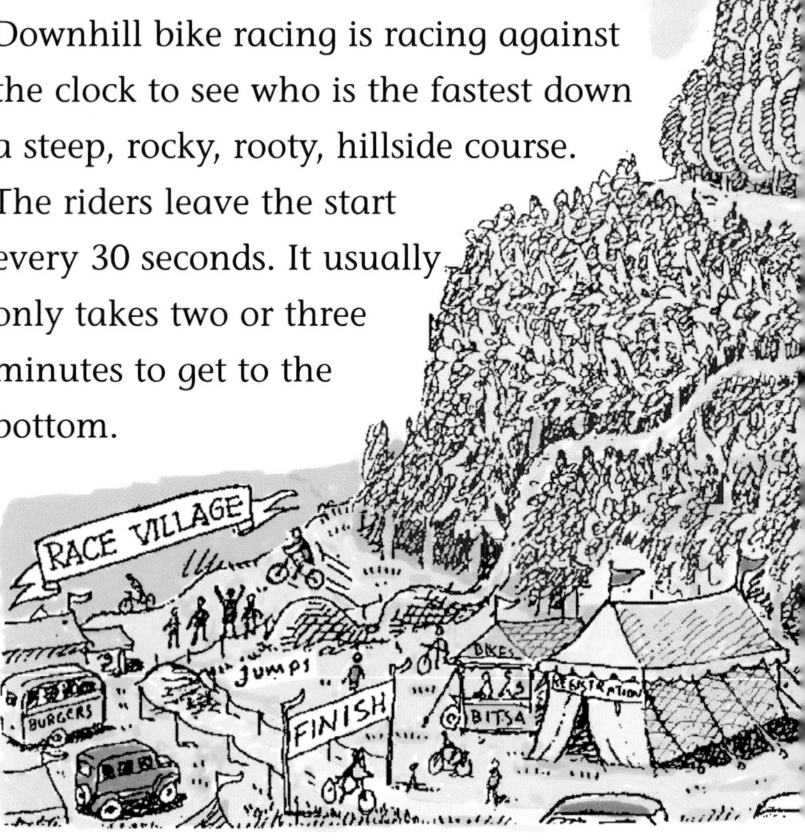
RACE VILLAGE
JUMPS
FINISH
BURGERS
BIKES
BITSA
REGISTRATION

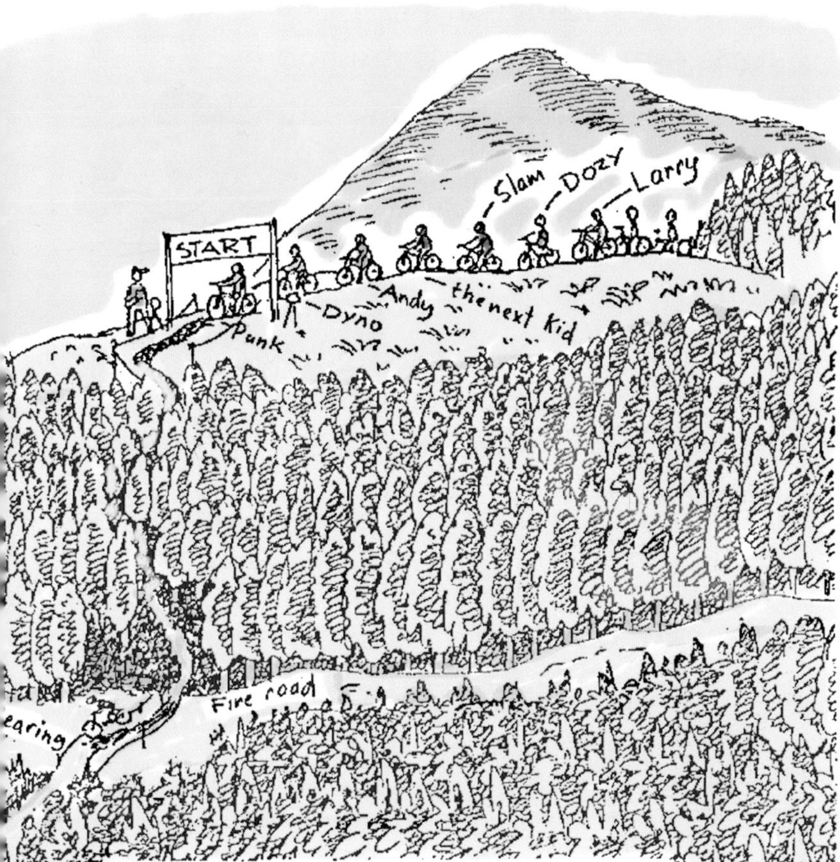
START
Slam
Dozy
Larry
Andy
the next Kid
Dyno
Punk
Fire road

Dozy loves gadgets. While we were waiting to start, he got out his stopwatch and binoculars so that he could time the first few riders crossing the road.

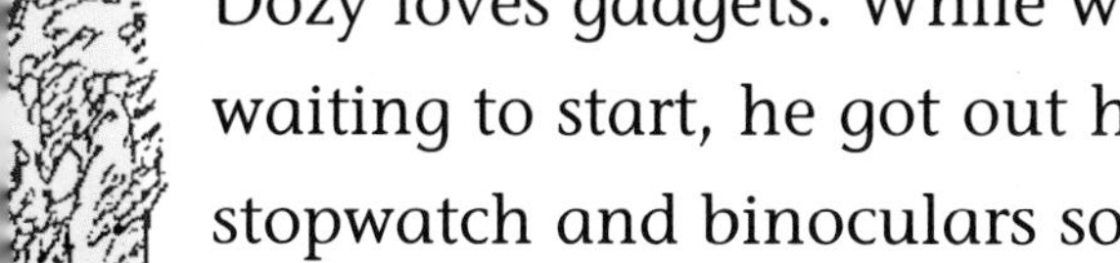
TOYARU
VADOR
FLEK

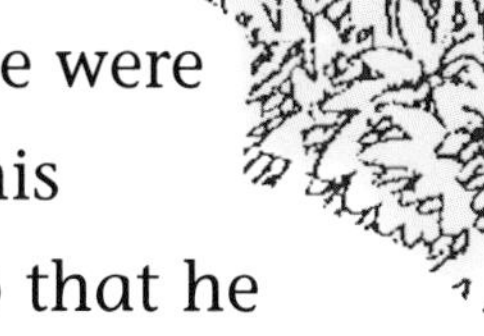
6

Punk, Dyno, Andy, and the next kid all went down. Then it was my turn. I went up to the start. I was excited. With my mud tires, I was definitely going to win this race.

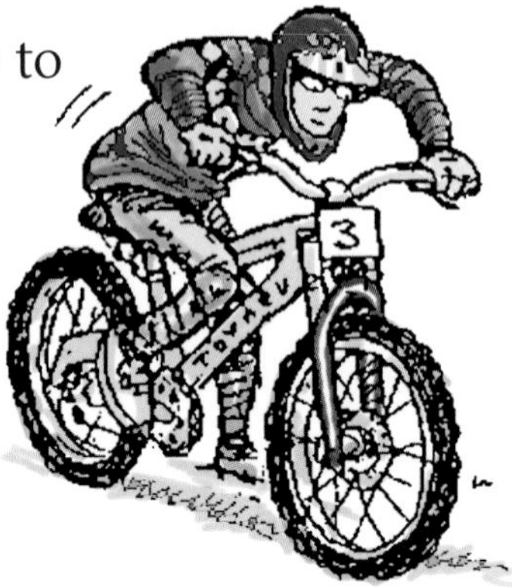
3

And then . . .

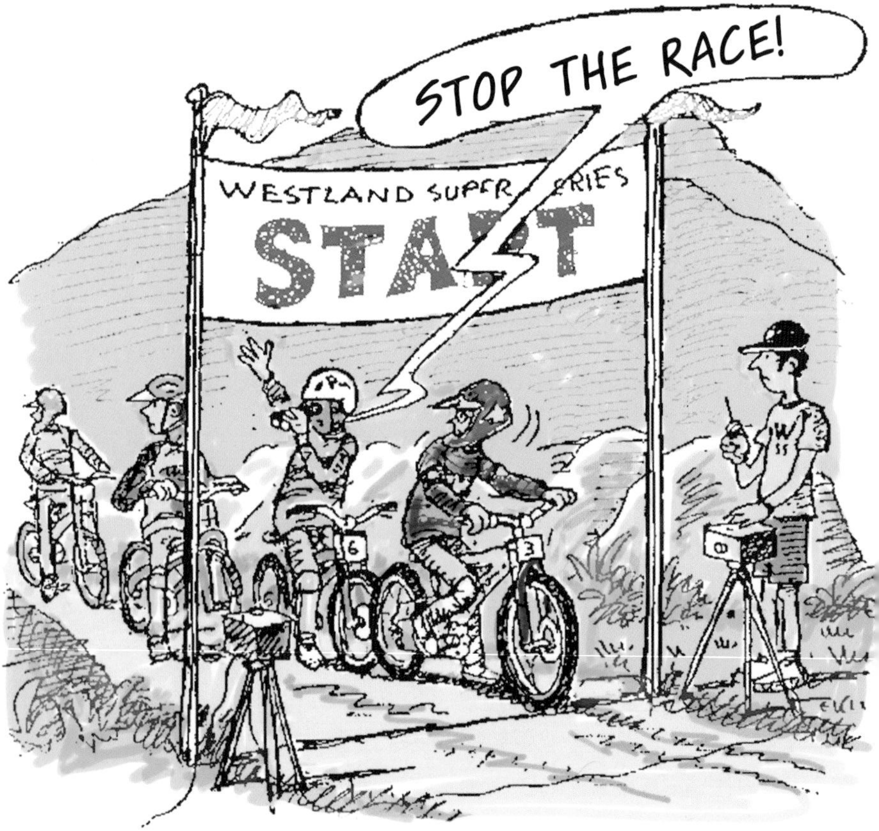
STOP THE RACE!
WESTLAND SUPER SERIES
START
6
3

Dozy was still looking through his binoculars.

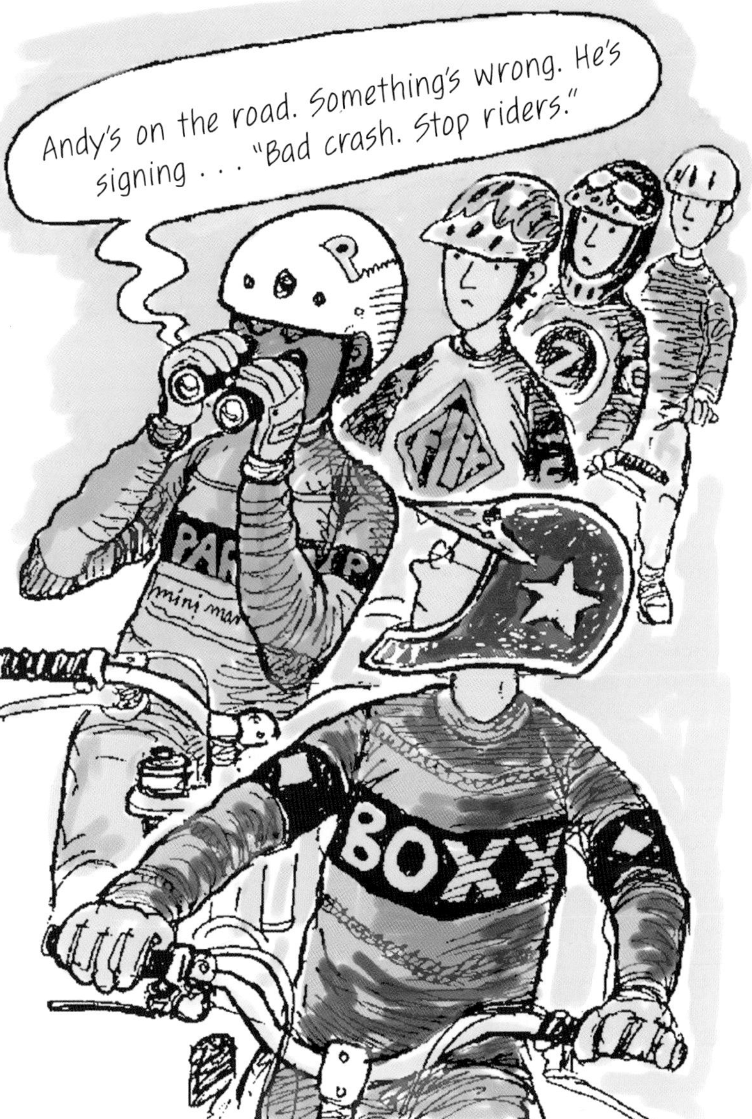
Andy's on the road. Something's wrong. He's signing . . . "Bad crash. Stop riders."
PA
mini mar
BOXX

Later, Andy told us what had happened.

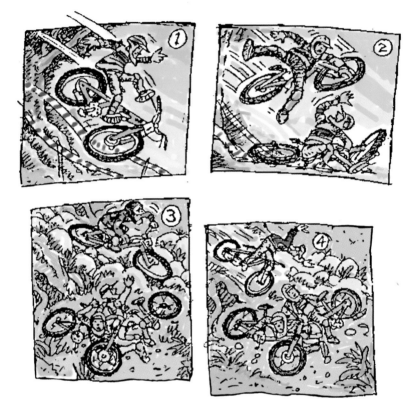

1. Punk fell.
2. Dyno fell on Punk.
3. Passing them was too hard.
4. The next kid fell.

5. There was a pile-up.

6. Andy didn't know what to do.

7. He rode to the clearing.

8. Then he signed to Dozy to stop the race.

Andy had decided to stop his own run because it might help save our runs. And it worked. When the crash was cleared up, the race restarted.

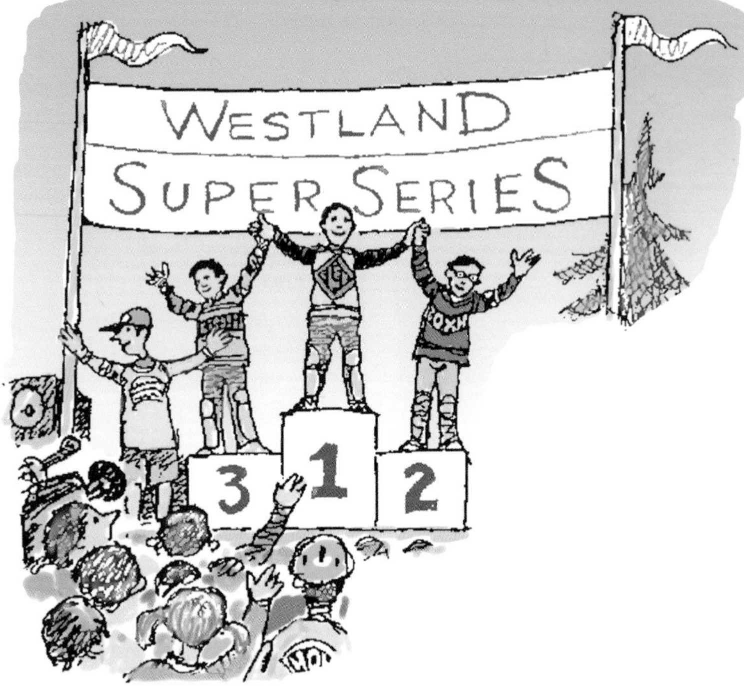
WESTLAND
SUPER SERIES
3
1
2

Larry took first that day, I took second, and Dozy got third. Fiona won the girls' race. Andy did not finish.

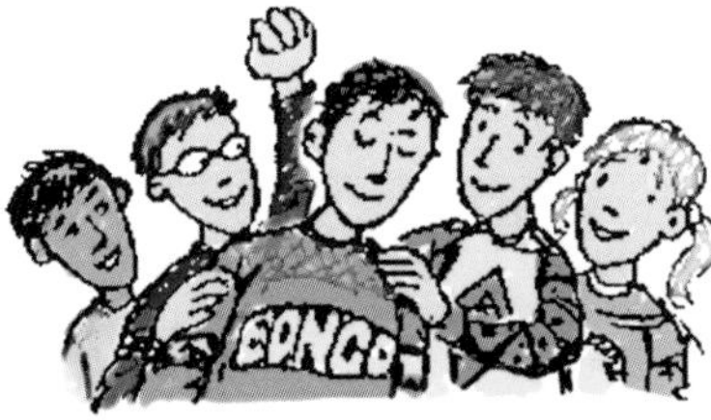

We all thanked him because things could have been very different.

He signed to us, "You'd do the same thing for me, wouldn't you?"

And we all said:

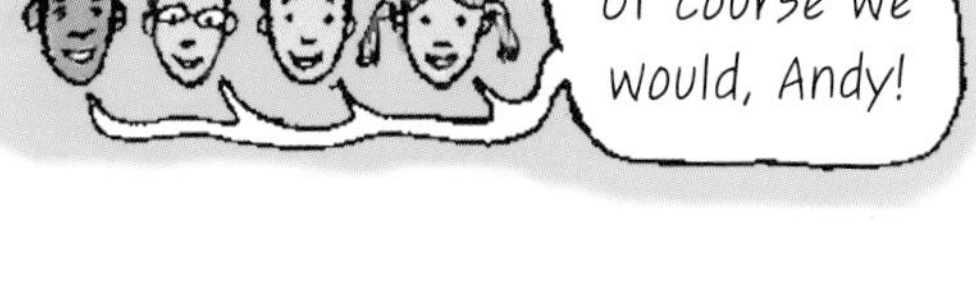
Of course we would, Andy!

About the Author and Illustrator

Robin and Chris Lawrie wrote the *Ridge Riders* books together, and Robin illustrated them. Their inspiration for these books is their son. They wanted to write books that he would find interesting. Many of the *Ridge Riders* books are based on adventures he and his friends had while biking.

Robin and Chris live in England, and will soon be moving to a big, old house that is also home to sixty bats.

Glossary

binoculars (buh-NOK-yuh-lurz)—an instrument that makes distant things look nearer

determined (di-TUR-mind)—if you are determined, you have made a decision to do something

distractions (diss-TRAK-shuhnz)—things that take your mind off of what you are doing

gadgets (GAJ-its)—tools that do specific jobs

link (LINGK)—one of the separate rings that make up a chain. A **link** can also mean a connection between people, or the thing that joins people together.

reaction (ree-AK-shuhn)—a response

rivals (RYE-vuhlz)—someone you compete with

sign language (SINE LANG-gwij)—a language in which hand gestures, facial expressions, and body movements are used instead of speech

spokes (SPOKES)—one of the thin rods that connect the rim of a wheel to the center

timed (TIMED)—measured with a clock

Internet Sites

Do you want to know more about subjects related to this book? Or are you interested in learning about other topics? Then check out FactHound, a fun, easy way to find Internet sites.

Our investigative staff has already sniffed out great sites for you!

Here's how to use FactHound:

1. Visit *www.facthound.com*

2. Select your grade level.

3. To learn more about subjects related to this book, type in the book's ISBN number: **9781434204837**.

4. Click the **Fetch It** button.

FactHound will fetch the best Internet sites for you!

Discussion Questions

1. What is a chain reaction? Can you think of an example of a chain reaction from your own life?

2. How did the Ridge Riders stop the chain reaction? Could they have done something about it earlier? What could they have done?

3. When the Ridge Riders were upset with each other, they didn't do well in the race. Why do you think that happened? If you're distracted by something, what are some ways to focus on the thing you have to do?

Writing Prompts

1. Andy gives up on his race because he knows it might make his friends win. Has anyone ever done something like that for you, or have you done something like that for someone else? Write about it.

2. Have you ever gotten upset with teammates the way that the Ridge Riders do in this book? Write about that. How did you solve the problem?

3. Slam imagines that he and his friends are each links in a chain. Can you think of something that would describe the way that you and your friends are? What object are you like? Why? Write about it!

More downhill fun . . .

SNOW BORED
GRAPHIC NOVEL
Robin & Chris Lawrie
STONE ARCH
Realistic Fiction

Snow Bored

The Ridge Riders are bored. So much snow has fallen on their mountain biking practice hill that they can't ride. Luckily, Dozy has a great idea. He turns an old skateboard and a pair of sneakers into a snowboard. Before long, everyone is snowboarding!

WHITE LIGHTNING
GRAPHIC NOVEL
Robin & Chris Lawrie
STONE ARCH
Realistic Fiction

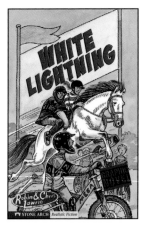

White Lightning

On the day of the last race, Slam gets a flat tire and has to race back home to get his spare, and he only has 50 minutes! When the bridge gets washed out, how will he ever make it back to finish the race?

. . . with the Ridge Riders!

RADAR RIDERS
GRAPHIC NOVEL
Robin & Chris Lawrie
STONE ARCH Realistic Fiction

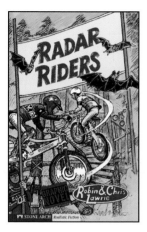

Radar Riders

When a new course is too hard for Larry, the Ridge Riders put together a soundtrack to accompany the course. Their techno-wizardry seems like a great idea . . . until they run into some unexpected twists and turns.

TREETOP TRAUMA
GRAPHIC NOVEL
Robin & Chris Lawrie
STONE ARCH Realistic Fiction

Treetop Trauma

The Ridge Riders have to save their racing hill from being bulldozed! They sign a petition, stage a protest, and even organize a hunger strike to try to stop the heavy machinery from ruining their hill. Will their hunger for biking be greater than their hunger for cheeseburgers?

Check out more Stone Arch Books graphic novels!

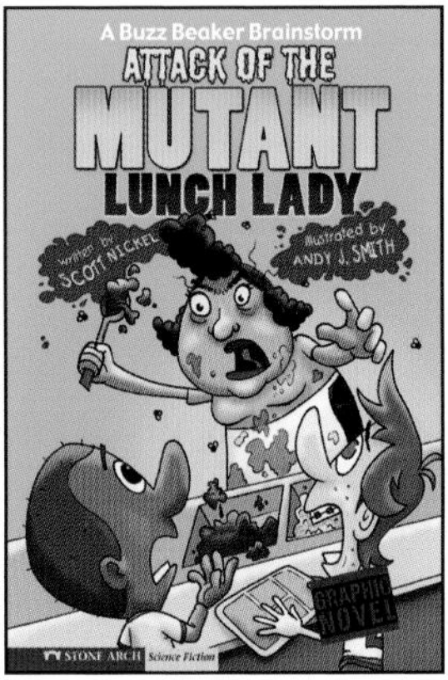
A Buzz Beaker Brainstorm
ATTACK OF THE MUTANT LUNCH LADY
written by SCOTT NICKEL
illustrated by ANDY J. SMITH
GRAPHIC NOVEL
STONE ARCH Science Fiction

Attack of the Mutant Lunch Lady by Scott Nickel

Brainy Buzz Beaker thought nothing could be grosser than cafeteria food — until the school's lunch lady turned into a mutant blob of mystery meat. Now, Buzz and his best friend, Larry, must discover a way to stop the Cafeteria Creature!

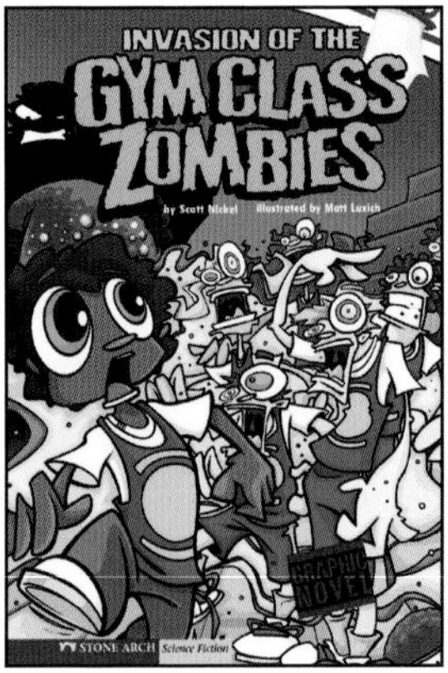
INVASION OF THE GYM CLASS ZOMBIES
by Scott Nickel
illustrated by Matt Luxich
GRAPHIC NOVEL
STONE ARCH Science Fiction

Invasion of the Gym Class Zombies by Scott Nickel

With the evil scientist Dr. Brainium in jail, Trevor thought his zombie-busting days were over. Then his new teacher, Mr. Brawnium, turned the whole gym class into radio-controlled jocks!